THE CAT IN THE HAT
Knows a Lot About That!™

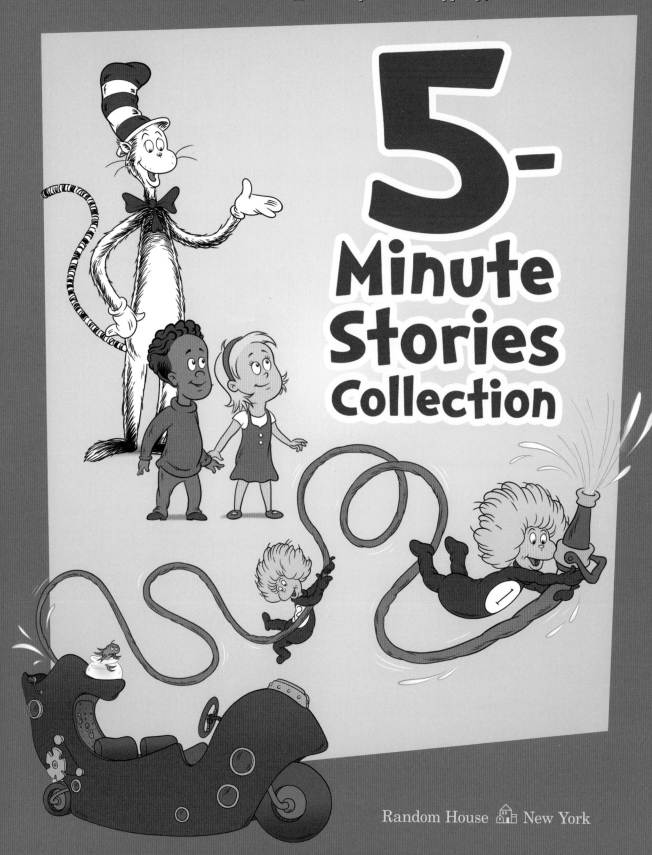

5-Minute Stories Collection

Random House 🏠 New York

Visit us on the Web!
Seussville.com
rhcbooks.com

Educators and librarians, for a variety of teaching tools, visit us at RHTeachersLibrarians.com

Library of Congress Cataloging-in-Publication Data is available upon request.
ISBN 978-0-593-37354-5 (trade) — ISBN 978-0-593-37355-2 (ebook)

MANUFACTURED IN CHINA

10 9 8 7 6 5 4 3 2 1

Random House Children's Books supports the First Amendment and celebrates the right to read.

CONTENTS

Step This Way

adapted by Tish Rabe

from a script by Graham Ralph

illustrated by Tom Brannon

"These shoes are cool," said Nick.
"But as you can see,
 they may fit your dad,
 but they're too big for me."

"When I wear my mom's shoes,"
 said Sally, "I fall.
 Her shoes are too big,
 and my feet are too small."

"Shoe trouble?" the Cat said.
"Well, I have some news.
Not everyone's feet can
fit in the same shoes.

"Feet come in all sizes,
and soon you'll see that
some are flippy, some flappy,
and some feet are flat.

"Want to see some neat feet?
Well, today I'll take you
to a faraway place:
Bing-Bungle-Ba-Boo!
It's a wonderful place
full of friends you will meet.
And each of them has,
oh, such different feet!"

In minutes they landed
in Bing-Bungle-Ba-Boo,
right by a lake,
and the Cat called, "Yoo-hoo!"

"Hello there, Cat! Welcome
  to my lake," said a duck.
"Emily!" cried the Cat.
"There you are! We're in luck!

"Meet Emily, one of
  my friends," said the Cat.
"As you see, her two feet
  are all flippy and flat."

"It's true," said the duck.
"My feet are long and wide.
Let's swim and I'll race you
to the other side."

The kids tried their best,
but soon Sally said,
"We've fallen behind.
Emily's way ahead!"

"She won," said the Cat,
"and we came in last.
Her feet push the water
so she can swim fast.

"Duck feet are perfect
for swimming, it's true.
With my Flipper-ma-zippers
we can swim fast, too."

They swam really fast
and crossed the finish line.
Then they heard a voice call,
"Do you have feet like mine?"

"Nick and Sally," the Cat said,
"I'd like you to meet
  Mikey the Lemur,
  who hangs by his feet."

"Our feet aren't like yours,"
  said Nick. "Not at all.
  If we hung by our feet,
  I'm afraid we would fall."

"I have lemur feet,"
  said the Cat, "just for you.
  Now you can hang
  the way Mikey can do."

Before the kids knew it,
they were up in a tree.
"I can hang like a lemur,"
said Nick. "Look at me!"

"Try this!" Mikey said.
"You will think that it's neat.
You can hang upside down
just by using your feet."

"Lemurs are great climbers,"
a voice said, "but see?
Nobody is better
at climbing than me!"

"Greg the Gecko!" the Cat said.
"We're glad to see you.
Geckos have feet
that can stick just like glue."

"Tiny hairs," said Greg,
"help my feet to grip.
These hairs let me hold on
so I do not slip."

The Cat passed out gecko feet.
Nick said, "This is tricky.
I can't move at all.
My feet are too sticky."

"Look!" said the gecko.
"I'll show you my trick—
press and peel, peel and press,
and your feet will not stick."

They pressed and they peeled,
and the gecko was right.
They walked upside down,
and their feet held on tight.

"I can walk like a gecko!"
said Nick. "Who would guess
you can walk upside down
if you peel and you press?

"Try duck feet for swimming,
and lemurs' for gripping.
The feet of a gecko
will keep you from slipping.

"But, Sally, I think that
when we get back home,
I'll return your dad's shoes
and just wear . . . my own!"

A Long Winter's Nap

adapted by Tish Rabe

from a script by Ken Cuperus

illustrated by Aristides Ruiz and Joe Mathieu

"It's dark out,
but I'm wide awake," Sally said.
"Me too," said Nick.
"I'm not ready for bed."

They tried reading a story.
They tried counting sheep.
Then they heard a voice call,
"You should go to Gleep Sneep!"

The kids knew that voice.
The kids knew that hat.
There was only one Cat
who said "Gleep Sneep" like that!

"We're sleepy," said Nick,
"but we're wide awake, too."
"Don't worry," the Cat said.
"I know what to do.

"To the Whispering Wood
we must go! That is where
you can meet my dear friend,
good old Boris the Bear.

"He lives deep in the woods
to the east of Gleep Sneep,
and he knows lots of ways
to help you fall asleep."

They soon landed inside of
the Whispering Wood.
Nick asked, "Should we whisper?"
The Cat said, "We should."

"Cat, is that you?" Boris said
with a smile.
"Haven't seen you in ages.
It's been a long while.

"I'm so glad to see you,
but what brings you here?
It's freezing in Gleep Sneep
this time of the year."

"We need help," said Sally.
"We can't get to sleep."
"Well," said Boris, "you'll find
  lots of help in Gleep Sneep!

"When it comes to sleeping,
  I know every trick."
"We can use all the help
  we can get," answered Nick.

"Do you know," Boris asked,
"about my situation? I'm just
  getting ready
  for my hibernation.

"It's a bear's winter nap. It's a
  very long thing. I go to sleep in
  the fall and wake up in the
  spring."

Then Boris saw something
and started to shake.
"Oh no," he cried. "Look!
I just saw a snowflake!

"As soon as I see one,
I have to get going.
I have to start sleeping
before it starts snowing!"

"We'll help you," said Sally,
"get ready to rest.
When it comes to helping,
we three are the best."

"Thank you!" said Boris.
"Come on, follow me
to my snuggly home under
the roots of this tree.

"I need a big pile that's at least three feet deep of twigs, leaves, and branches before I can sleep."

They found armfuls of twigs, leaves, and branches, and then they built a deep pile inside Boris's den.

Then suddenly they heard
a very strange rumble.
"My stomach," said Boris,
"is starting to grumble.

"I now need to eat
a meal fit for a king.
It will be my last meal
until sometime next
spring."

The Cat called in the cooks!
(Thing One and Thing Two.)
"They will cook," said the Cat,
"a fine dish just for you!"

So those cooks started cooking
and they did not stop. Nuts
and Berries Supreme with
leaves sprinkled on top!
Boris ate the whole thing.

That bear ate every bite.
Then he said, "Very soon,
you can tuck me in tight.

"But before I can sleep,
there's one thing I must do.
I must go to the bathroom
and you can go, too."

Boris soon settled down.
"Now I'm sleepy," he said.
"Here's a pillow of leaves
to put under my head.

"I'm ready to start
to hibernate.
I'll see you in springtime.
I'll miss you, but . . .

". . . WAIT!

"I can't hibernate yet in my
den in Gleep Sneep.
I promised to help both of
you fall asleep!"

"I have an idea," said the Cat.
"I will try to sing to you a
nighty-night lullaby."

So they all snuggled down
by the light of the moon,
and the Cat in the Hat
began singing a tune.

"When the weather turns cold
and the snow grows deep,
a bear curls up for a very
long sleep.

"The name of this sleep
is hibernation, and it takes
lots of careful preparation."

"Hear that?" whispered Sally.
"Your song worked so well.
Boris is snoring! He's asleep,
I can tell.

"He went to the bathroom.
He's comfy and fed.
Now we should go home
and get ready for bed."

Back home Nick said,
"Now we can sleep the night
   through, but we can't hibernate
   like a bear gets to do."

They got under the covers.
The Cat yawned. "Good night!"
Then he reached out his tail,
and he turned out the light.

Now You See Me...

adapted by Tish Rabe

based on a television script by Katherine Standford

illustrated by Christopher Moroney

Nick said, "It's vacation!
And we have all week
to play games and have fun.
Want to play hide-and-seek?"

"You count and I'll hide,"
Sally said. "And you'll see—
I'll hide so well that
you'll never find me!"

Sally looked till she found
a good hiding spot.
". . . Ten!" Nick called out.
"Coming! Ready or not!"

Where was Sally hiding?
In less than a minute,
Nick ran to the wheelbarrow
and found Sally in it!

"Hide-and-seek!" cried the Cat.
"Oh, I'm so glad I came!
 The counting! The hiding!
 It's my favorite game!"

"It's great!" Nick agreed.
 Sally said as she sighed,
"But Nick always finds me
 wherever I hide."

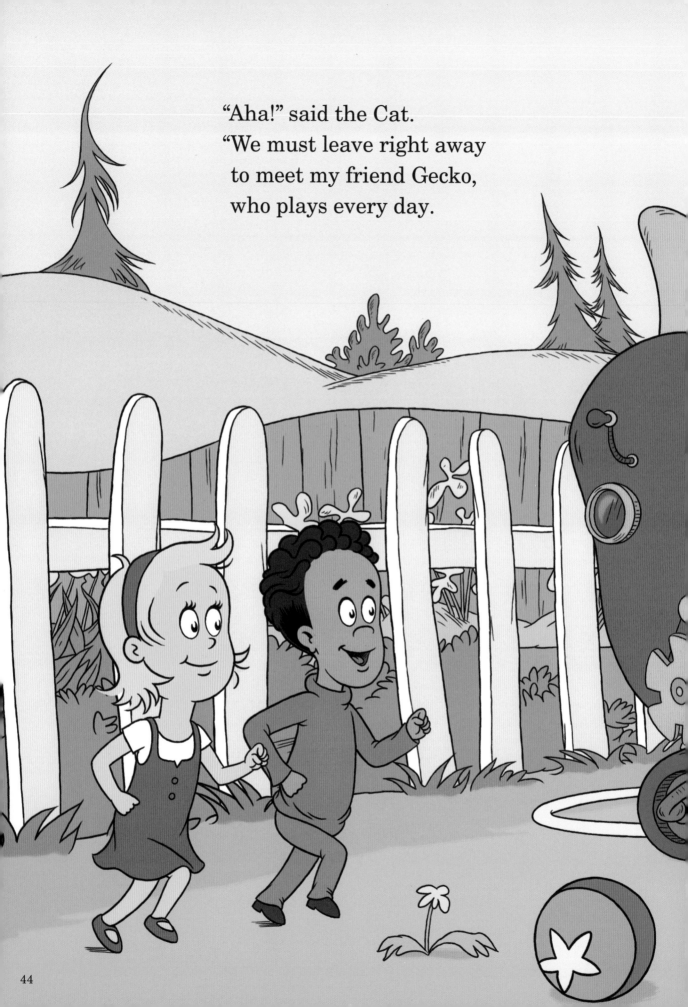

"Aha!" said the Cat.
"We must leave right away
to meet my friend Gecko,
who plays every day.

"He hides in the day
and also at night.
It helps him stay safe
to keep out of sight."

So they flew to the jungle.
It was steamy and hot.
"My friend," said the Cat,
"is not easy to spot.

"Cam-ou-flage helps him hide.
It is his hiding trick."
"Cam-ou-*what*? I don't know
what that word means!" said Nick.

"I'll explain," said the Cat.
"Camouflage is the way
  some animals stay
  out of sight every day.

"Camouflage helps them hide
  so they will not be found.
  It helps them blend in
  with whatever's around.

"That Gecko blends in.
He's not easy to see."
"Hello!" Gecko called.
"Are you looking for me?

"My tail looks leaf-like
and my skin is light brown.
I'm hanging right here in
this tree upside down!"

"Could you show us," asked Sally,
"how to hide like you do?
 We want to learn how
 to use camouflage, too!"

"In the jungle," said Gecko,
"your clothes are too bright.
 You need to blend in
 so you stay out of sight."

"We can't hide dressed like this,"
said Nick. "What to do?"
"You need help," said the Cat,
"from Thing One and Thing Two!"

"Can you help us," asked Sally,
"look leafy and green?
If we look like the jungle,
we'll never be seen."

So, before the kids knew it,
they got a surprise—
Things One and Two made
them the perfect disguise!

"Mr. Gecko," said Nick,
"you can hide, it is true.
But can you find us
when we're hiding from *you*?"

"Of course!" Gecko said,
   but when he looked around,
   those camouflaged kids
   were nowhere to be found!

He looked in the shadows
   and looked in the light.
   They were hiding so well
   they were nowhere in sight.

Then all of a sudden
a tree started to wiggle.
"Wait!" Gecko said.
"I just heard someone giggle!

"Out here in the jungle,"
he said with a smile,
"the trees haven't giggled
in quite a long while."

"Nick," Sally asked,
"when I was hiding today,
how did you find where
I was right away?"

"Well," Nick said, "finding
you wasn't hard.
Your dress was the only pink
thing in my yard."

"Hide-and-seek," said the Cat,
"is so much fun to play.
I could play it with Gecko
and you every day.

"But we have to go now.
We'll be back soon, I know.
Goodbye, Gecko!
Oh . . . Gecko?

"NOW where did he go?"

Planet Name Game

adapted by Tish Rabe

based on a television script by Patrick Granleese

illustrated by Tom Brannon

One day the Cat said,
"Today we will fly
and see all the planets
way up in the sky.

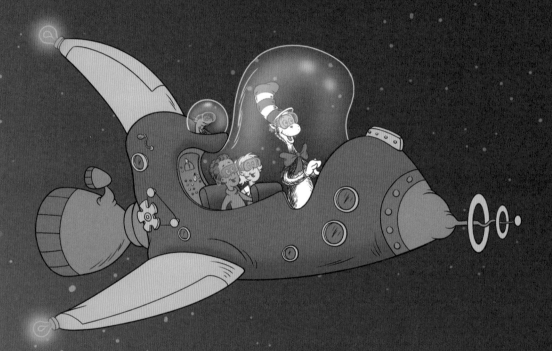

"There are eight planets
that circle the sun.
We can name them all
and have lots of fun.

"First stop is the sun.
Look! Here we are!
Have I told you that
the sun is a star?

"Up in the sky
it may look like a dot.
When we get close,
you can feel it is HOT!

"The first planet we see
is closest to the sun.
It is Mercury.
It is the smallest one.

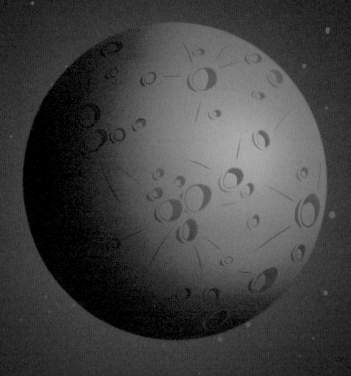

"We named one planet.
Now what do we do?
Now we blast off for
planet number two!

"This planet is Venus.
It never rains here.
It is dusty and dry
every day of the year.

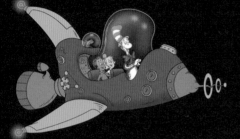

"This planet is Earth.
We can easily see
why it is called the Blue Planet.
It is Planet Three.

"It has lots of oceans
that make it look blue.
I love this planet!
I bet you do, too!

"Now we will fly
    way up past some stars
    to the next planet,
    the one we call Mars."

"I know that Mars is
    the Red Planet," Nick said.
"And I can see why.
    It really *is* red!"

"Jupiter," the Cat said,
"is fifth from the sun.
As you can see,
it's the biggest one.

"We can see it is big
when we fly beside it.
The other planets
could all fit inside it!

"This planet is Saturn.
We can see two things.
It's the second biggest
and it has bright rings.

"It is the sixth planet.
There are only two more.
Oh! I think space is
such fun to explore!

"Next is Uranus (YUR-uh-nus).
It has rings, too.
There is just one planet
left to show you.

"This planet is Neptune.
It is Planet Eight.

"We did it! Hooray!
This name game is great!

"We named them all.
Our name game is fun.
We can do it again
and start with Planet One!

"Mercury and Venus
were such fun to see.
Earth is where we live.
It is Planet Three.

"We named Mars and then
we named Jupiter, too.
Saturn was the sixth
planet I showed you.

"Uranus, then Neptune . . .
Our name game is done.
Unless—we play it again
and start with . . .

"... the sun!"

Hooray for Hair!

adapted by Tish Rabe

from a script by Karen Moonah

illustrated by Tom Brannon

"Crazy Hair Day in school
is tomorrow," said Nick.
"We need crazy hair
and we both need it quick.

"Short on the top?
Or long on each side?
Straight, wavy, or curly?
I just can't decide."

"Did you say crazy hair?"
said the Cat. "Jump in back.
Today I will take you
to visit a yak.

"His hair is yak-tastic.
It's shaggy and thick."
"Sounds like a really cool
hairstyle," said Nick.

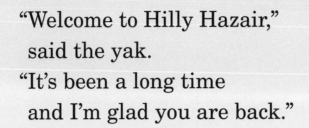

"Welcome to Hilly Hazair,"
said the yak.
"It's been a long time
and I'm glad you are back."

"You have nice hair,
Mister Yak," Sally said.
"I wish I had hair
just like yours on my head."

"Please," said the yak,
"just call me Yancy.
My hair is shaggy,
but not very fancy."

"If it's yak hair you want,"
said the Cat, "I'll show you
just what my new
Wig-o-lator can do!

"It springs and it sings,
and in just a short while,
it will give both of you
a super hairstyle.
You'll love your new look!"
The Cat lowered the hood.
"Oh boy!" whispered Nick.
"This is gonna be good."

The Cat pushed a button
and the thing started dinging.
Buzzers were buzzing.
Bells began ringing.
"It tickles!" said Nick.
"This is fun!" Sally said.
"It is putting a wig
on the top of my head."

In less than a minute
both Sally and Nick
had hair like a yak's.
It was shaggy and thick.
"You look great!" said Yancy.
"It's easy to see,
with your thick, shaggy hair,
you two look just like me."

"It's cold here in
Hilly Hazair," Sally said.
"The only thing warm
is the top of my head.
It's fun to have thick hair
like Yancy has got,
but in summer this thick hair
would really be hot."

"Then you'd need hair
   of a much different sort.
   Like my friend," said the Cat,
"who has hair that is short.

"I will take you
   to Blue-Puddle-a-Roo
   to meet Celia the Seal.
   She can't wait to meet you."

"Hey, Cat!" cried Celia.
"I've been waiting all week."
"Celia," said the Cat,
"has short hair that is sleek."

"Jump in, kids," said Celia.
"The water is fine.
If you're a fur seal,
you need short hair like mine."

"The water's so cold,"
said Sally. "How do you
swim all day long
in Blue-Puddle-a-Roo?"

"I've two layers of hair,"
Celia said. "This is why
though the top one gets wet,
my skin still stays dry.

"I just go jump in
the water, and poof!
I'm warm because
my hair's waterproof."

"On my Wig-o-lator,"
the Cat said, "this wheel
will spin to give you
the hair of a seal!"

"It feels good," said Sally.
"But I just don't know
if yak hair or seal hair
is how we should go.

"Long hair is warmer,
 but short hair is neat."
"Come on!" said the Cat.
"There's one more friend to meet.
 Here in Poki Moloki
 lives a good friend of mine.
 His name is Quincy.
 He's a fine porcupine.
 Quincy has talent.
 He's really the best.
 He can fluff up his quills
 in a porcupine crest."

"Hello, Cat," said Quincy.
"Be careful. Stand back!
My sharp quills protect me
from any attack.
My quills are like hair,
but they're sharp to the touch.
Do you have quills, Nick?"
Nick said, "No, not so much."
"To the Wig-o-lator!" the Cat cried.
"Don't run! Get in line.
And you'll soon have quills
like a fine porcupine.
This is a hairstyle
that everyone likes.
Soon you will each have . . .

". . . a head full of spikes!"
"We look pretty sharp,"
   Sally said with a smile.
"But I'm not sure that
   porcupine quills are our style."

"It's time to head back,"
   said the Cat. "So let's fly!"
"See you later!" said Quincy.
   The kids called, "Goodbye!"

"Cat," Sally said,
"before we went to Hazair,
I'd never seen so many
new kinds of hair.
Hair keeps yaks warm
and keeps a seal dry.
Quills protect Quincy,
who's such a nice guy."

"You're right," said the Cat.
"Hair is not just for show.
It can help you stay warm
in the cold winter snow.
It keeps porcupines
from becoming a meal
and helps keep you dry
if you are a fur seal."

"For Crazy Hair Day," said Nick,
"what we'll do
is have yak hair and seal hair
and porcupine, too!
Crazy Hair Day is
going to be great.
Let's both get up early
so we won't be late."

"How was Crazy Hair Day
today?" asked the Cat.
"I wore," said Nick,
"a yak-seal-porcupine hat.
Having yak-seal-porcupine
hair wasn't bad,
but now I'll go back
to the hair . . .
that I had!"

A Tale About Tails

adapted by Tish Rabe

based on a television script by Pete Sauder

illustrated by Tom Brannon

"You did it!" said Sally.
"Believe it or not,
 you taped the tail
 in just the right spot!"

"Paper tails are okay," said Nick,
"but how would it feel
 if, instead of paper,
 we had tails that were real?"

"Tails are great!" cried the Cat.
"Mine helps me beat the heat.
It fans my back.
It makes a great seat.
I use it to jump rope
and turn out the light.
It pulls down the shade
in my bedroom at night."

"I love my tail, too!"
  said the Fish with a *splish*.
"I think it's the perfect
  tail for a fish."
"It's true," said the Cat.
"His tail helps him swim.
  A fish-swishy tail
  is the right one for him!"

"A tail," Sally said,
"looks like lots of fun,
  but if *I* got a tail,
  how would I choose one?"
"I've got it!" the Cat said.
"I know what to do
  to find out which tail
  is the right one for you!

"To the Thinga-ma-jigger!
And we will set sail
for the faraway Jungle
of Wagga-tag-tail.
The tails you will see there
you'll never believe,
and once we get there,
you will not want to leave!"

Off to Wagga-tag-tail
they went, and once there
they started looking
for tails everywhere.
"Tails can be short,
curly, fluffy, or long.
First, we'll meet a monkey
whose tail is quite strong."

"Hello!" called the monkey.
"Up here! Look at me!
With my tail, I can swing
branch to branch, tree to tree."
"Your tail," Sally said,
"helps you fly through the air,
but we don't have tails,
so we can't get up there."

"I know," said the Cat,
"how to get tails for you.
I'll call on the help
of Thing One and Thing Two.
You will soon have the best
tails that you've ever seen
when they build you a . . .

". . . Tail-a-ma-fixer machine!
Just step inside it
and soon you will see
you can pick any tail
and the tails are all free."

Nick pushed a button
and said, "Monkey tails, please!
Sally and I want
to swing through the trees."
The Tail-a-ma-fixer
started to quake.
Lights started to flash
and it started to shake.
"Hold on!" Sally said.
And the next thing she knew . . .

. . . she had a tail like a monkey's—
and Nick had one, too!
"With our tails," Sally said,
"we can swing high and low
in the trees like a monkey.
Come on, Cat. Let's go!"

They were starting to swing
in the trees way up high
when they saw a big bird
that came flying on by.
"It's a quetzal," the Cat said,
"and take it from me—
he has one of the prettiest
tails we will see."

"His tail is so bright,"
  Sally said to the Cat.
"Can you get us tails
  just as pretty as that?"
"We have quetzal tails!" Nick said.
"They're bright blue and green.
  They're the prettiest tails
  that I've ever seen!"
They flew with the quetzal,
  then suddenly heard
  a sound that they knew
  was not made by a bird.

"Did you hear that?" asked Nick.
"I heard *shake, shake, shake, shake.*"
The Cat said, "That sound's from
the tail of a snake.
That's a rattlesnake,
and its tail makes a sound
to warn everyone
that a snake is around."

"Tails like that could come in
very handy," said Nick.
"I'll push the snake button
and get us some quick!

"Come on, Sally, let's shake
our tails like a snake.
It's easy to do. We just
shake, shake, shake, shake!"

"We've done a tail tour,"
the Cat said, "and have found
some are pretty, some handy,
and some make a sound.
A monkey's tail holds on,
and as you can see,
he needs his strong tail
to live up in a tree.

"A quetzal's tail looks
very pretty and bright.
When he flies through the sky,
it's a beautiful sight.

"A rattlesnake's tail
makes a sound you can hear.
It's this snake's way of warning
that danger is near.

"There are all kinds of tails,
fun, fancy, and fine,
but the tail I like most
in the whole world is . . . mine!"

The Tree Doctor

adapted by Tish Rabe

from a script by Bernice Vanderlaan

illustrated by Tom Brannon

"Breakfast!" called Sally.
"The pancakes are hot!
Let's find out how much
maple syrup we've got."

"Trees give sap to make syrup,"
said Nick, "but this one
is so small, we can't make
any syrup. No fun!"

"I smell pancakes!" the Cat cried.
"Oh, I hope I am right.
I love golden pancakes,
all fluffy and light,
with sweet maple syrup.

"Oh, pour me some, please!
It's my favorite thing
that we get from the trees."

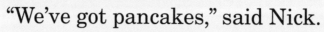

"We've got pancakes," said Nick.
"But unfortunately,
no sap to make syrup
from our maple tree."

"Not to worry!" the Cat said.
"Today I'll take you
 to meet the Tree Doctor.
 He'll know what to do.

"Meet Dr. Twiggles!
He takes care of trees.
He swings through the branches
and hangs by his knees!"

"Hello," said the doctor.
"Yes, it's up to me
to respond to and treat
every tree-mergency!

Dr. Twigberry Twiggles
2 Spruce Street
Wild Woolly Wood

If your pine is in pain or your oak's not OK,
call me night or day. I'll be there right away.

"Now, what brings you three
to the Wild Woolly Wood?"
"Our tree's not growing,"
answered Nick, "as it should."

"Little tree," said the doctor,
"how are you feeling?
Are your twigs in a twist?
Has your bark started peeling?

"Hmm . . . color's nice and dark.
Stem is not bumpy.
Branches aren't brittle.
Twigs are not lumpy.
But these leaves are drooping,
and that means, I'd say,
I should check your tree's roots
and do so right away."

"Check the roots?" Sally asked.
"How can you do that?"
"To the Thinga-ma-jigger!"
cried the Cat in the Hat.

"Flip the Thrilla-ma-driller,
and we'll see if it's ill.
If you've never seen tree roots,
well, soon we all will!"

"Look at that," said Nick.
"This really is neat.
 The roots of a tree
 are like a tree's feet."

"AbsoROOTly!" the Cat cried.
"I happen to know
 roots soak up food and water
 and help a tree grow."

"I've got it!" the doc said.
"Now I see why
   your tree isn't growing.
The soil is too dry."

"It needs water?" the Cat asked.
"I know what to do.
This is a job
   for Thing One and Thing Two!"

Those two Things jumped out,
and they gave a big yank
to the crank on the side
of the Thinga-ma-tank.

But they turned it too far
and they turned it too fast.
Water shot out in a
soaking-wet blast!

"Good job!" said the doc.
"But our work is not done.
 To get healthy, your tree
 needs to get lots of sun."

"I know!" cried the Cat.
"Your tree will feel right
 when my Brighta-ma-lighter
 gives it sunlight."

"Now just wait," said the doc.
"In forty years you can tap
your tree and make syrup
from the maple tree sap."

"Forty years!" said Nick.
"When our tree is that old,
our stack of pancakes
will REALLY be cold!"

"No problem!" said the doc.
"For I have right here
   some syrup I made
   in the spring of last year.

"And I have something else—
a bag of maple keys,
full of maple tree seeds
to grow even more trees."

Back home, Nick said,
"This syrup is good,
and I had lots of fun
in the Wild Woolly Wood."

"Eat up!" said the Cat.
"Then I need your help, please.
After breakfast let's go and plant . . .

". . . more maple trees!"

How Wet Can You Get?

adapted by Tish Rabe

from a script by Bruce Robb

illustrated by Aristides Ruiz and Joe Mathieu

"When it rains," Sally said,
"it's fun to get wet!"
"Let's see," laughed Nick,
"just how wet we can get!

"Let's jump in this puddle!"
When Sally said "Yes!"
they jumped in and soon
were a mud-covered mess!

Then the Thinga-ma-jigger flew in
and—*ker-splat!*—
mud splashed all over
the Cat in the Hat!

"We're a mess!" Sally said.
"We need to get clean."
"Yes," said the Cat.
"I can see what you mean.

"We'll go on a trip,
and I will show you
how to get clean
like the animals do!

"They get clean different ways,
and soon we'll see how.
Let's get out of the rain
and get going right now!

"Here's Carol the sparrow.
She knows a few things
about getting dirt off
her body and wings."

"First," said the sparrow,
"to get clean you must
cover yourself in a shower of dust.
Then flap your wings
to get dirt off you.
It works for us birds.
It will work for you, too!"
"I like flapping," said Nick,
"but I really don't see—
if we're covered in dust,
just how clean can we be?"

"Don't worry!" the Cat said.
"Next we'll meet some cats
   who clean with their tongues
   and do not wear hats.
   Meet Leona the Lion.
   When she licks her fur,
   her tongue is so rough
   it takes dirt right off her."

"That tickles!" laughed Sally.
"Their tongues do feel rough,
 but to get a kid clean
 I don't think that's enough."

"We're still really messy
 and muddy," Nick said.
"Let's go," said the Cat,
"and meet more friends up ahead.

"Hanna Hippo," the Cat said,
"will show us the way
 she gets mud and bugs off
 her skin every day."

"Join me," said Hanna,
"in this muddy pool.
 I don't get clean here.
 I just try to keep cool.

"I get clean when my friends
the oxpeckers begin
to peck all the mud
and the bugs off my skin.

"When they start pecking,
it's really ideal.
I get rid of the bugs,
and the birds get a meal."

So the oxpeckers started
their mud-pecking trick
and tried getting mud
off Sally and Nick.

"You know, Cat," said Nick,
"I have never heard
of a kid getting clean
with the help of a bird.

"We're not cats or hippos,
and I just can't see
how to get all this mud
off Sally and me."

"You're right," said the Cat.
"And I think that it's time
  to rid ourselves now
  of this dirt and this grime."

"We need something that works
  to get kids clean," said Nick.
"And we are so dirty,
  it needs to be quick!

"Hippos use birds to
 keep mud from sticking.
 Lions use tongues to
 get clean by licking.

"Sparrows use dust to get
 their feathers clean.
 But we need something else
 that we still haven't seen."

"I know!" said Sally.
"Let's hurry home now.
 There's a way to get clean,
 and I'll show you how!

"We won't stand in a shower
 or soak in a tub.
 We won't need any soap
 or a washcloth to scrub.

"We just need . . . a sprinkler!
 When we turn it on,
 in just a few minutes
 the mud will be gone!"

I Love the Nightlife!

adapted by Tish Rabe

from a script by Shawn Kalb

illustrated by Aristides Ruiz and Joe Mathieu

"Here we go!" cried the Cat.
"Stay awake! Hold on tight!
We are off to find critters
who stay up all night!

"Tonight's not for sleeping.
There's too much to do!
We are off to the Forest of Wagamaroo!

"I lost a hat there.
It flew off my head!"
"I'm sorry," yawned Nick.
"Now let's go back to bed."

"I'm sleepy," said Sally.
"Is there any way
we can look for your
hat during the *day*?"

"Tonight," said the Cat,
"we'll meet animals who
   hear, smell, and see better
   than you and I do!
   They are nocturnal animals.
   At nighttime they prowl."
   Suddenly, they heard
   the hoot of an owl!
"Whoooo are you?"
   asked the owl.
"And why are you here
   on one of the darkest
   nights of the year?"

"Excuse me," said Nick,
"but can you tell us why
   you wait till it's late
   before you start to fly?"
"I have big eyes," the owl said.
"When I fly at night,
   my eyes can see well
   even in the moonlight."

"I lost one of my hats," said the Cat,
"here last night.
  It's tall and it's red and
  has two stripes of white."
"I'm afraid," said the owl,
"though my eyesight is keen,
  your lost hat is one thing
  that I have not seen.
  Good night, and farewell!
  It is time to take wing!"
"It's so dark," Sally said,
"that I can't see a *thing*!"

The Cat cried, "Owl goggles!
We will each get a pair.
With them we'll be able
to see everywhere!"
"I'm looking," said Nick,
"but I don't see a hat.
Hey! I see something . . .
it looks like . . . a bat!"

"Mr. Bat," Sally said,
"we are glad to see you.
Have you seen a lost hat
here in Wagamaroo?"

"Not I," said the bat,
"but I'll tell you, my dear,
my bat ears hear sounds
some may find hard to hear."
"Can you help us?" asked Nick.
"Can you hear a lost hat?"
"I'm afraid," said the bat,
"even I can't do that!

"But . . . put on these bat ears
and then go out flying.
You will hear sounds
without even trying."

So they put on bat ears
and flew through the air,
but they still couldn't find
that Cat's hat anywhere!

"I can hear," Sally said,
"more than ever before,
but what kind of sounds
are we listening for?

"I hear chirping and slurping
and owl hoots, too,
but the sound of a hat
is not coming through."

Then they met an opossum
who was sniffing around.
"My nose," he explained,
"knows where food can be found."
"Do you think," Sally asked,
"since your nose works so well,
you could find the Cat's hat
with your keen sense of smell?"
"If I weren't so hungry,
I might," he replied.
"My nose must find dinner
to fill my inside."

"I know what to do!"
said the Cat. "Yes, indeed!"
Some opossum noses
are just what we need!"

"I found it!" Nick shouted.
"Although it is night,
I smell a red hat with
two stripes of white!"

"Hooray!" said the Cat.
"Now that my hat's back,
let's all celebrate with a
light late-night snack!"

Soon the bat and opossum
came to tell them goodbye,
while the owl went "whooo,"
flying high in the sky.

"It's morning!" the Cat said.
"Now they'll sleep all day through.
And I have a feeling . . .
you'll be asleep, too!"